Squirrel

Isabel Thomas

Heinemann
LIBRARY
Chicago, Illinois

WITHDRAWN

© 2014 Heinemann Library
an imprint of Capstone Global Library, LLC
Chicago, Illinois

To contact Capstone Global Library please phone 800-747-4992,
or visit our web site www.capstonepub.com

Edited by Dan Nunn, Rebecca Rissman, and Helen Cox
Cannons
Designed by Tim Bond
Original illustrations © Capstone Global Library Ltd 2014
Picture research by Mica Brancic
Production by Helen McCreath
Originated by Capstone Global Library Ltd
Printed and bound in China

17 16 15 14 13
10 9 8 7 6 5 4 3 2 1

Library of Congress Cataloging-in-Publication Data
Thomas, Isabel, 1980- author.
  Squirrel / Isabel Thomas.
    pages cm.—(City safari)
  Includes bibliographical references and index.
  ISBN 978-1-4329-8809-8 (hb)—ISBN 978-1-4329-8816-6 (pb) 1.
Gray squirrel—Juvenile literature. 2. Squirrels—Behavior—Juvenile
literature. 3. Urban animals—Juvenile literature. I. Title.

SB994.S67T46 2014
599.36'2—dc23   2013017409

Acknowledgments
The author and publisher are grateful to the following for
permission to reproduce copyright material: Alamy pp. 11 (©
Dizzy), 14 (© David Mabe), 18 (© Thom Moore), 19 (© Richard
Newton), 23 den (© Dizzy), 23 loft insulation (© Richard Newton),
23 mate (© Thom Moore); FLPA pp. 9 (David Tipling), 13 (Bill
Coster), 15 (Erica Olsen), 17 (Wayne Hutchinson), 21 (S & D & K
Maslowski), 23 predator (Wayne Hutchinson); Getty Images p.
4 (Tim Graham); Naturepl.com pp. 6 inset (© Bruno D'Amicis),
6 main & 7 (both © Warwick Sloss), 10 (© Doug Wechsler), 16
(© Rolf Nussbaumer), 20 (© Andrew Cooper), 23 drey (© Doug
Wechsler); Shutterstock pp. 5 (© ivvv1975) 6 (© Tom Reichner),
8 (© Yannick FEL), 12 (© Paul Orr), 23 fungi (© James Ac), 23
sense (© S.Cooper Digital).

Front cover photograph of a squirrel reproduced with permission
of Shutterstock (© Photomika-com). Back cover photograph of a
squirrel having a meal of bird seed reproduced with permission
of Shutterstock (© Paul Orr).

We would like to thank Michael Bright for his invaluable help in
the preparation of this book.

Every effort has been made to contact copyright holders of any
material reproduced in this book. Any omissions will be rectified
in subsequent printings if notice is given to the publisher.

Warning!

Never touch wild animals
or their homes. Some wild
animals carry diseases.
Scared animals may bite
or scratch you. Never hold
food for a squirrel to eat.
It may bite your finger
by mistake.

Note about spotter icon

Your eyes, ears,
and nose can tell you if a
squirrel is nearby. Look for
these clues as you read the
book, and find out more on
page 22.

Contents

Some words are shown in bold, **like this**.
You can find them in the glossary on page 23.

Who Has Been Spotted Stealing Picnic Food?

Gray fur. Short front legs. A bushy tail. It's a gray squirrel!

Pets are not the only animals that live in towns and cities.

red-brown patches

bushy tail

white belly

short front legs

long claws

Many wild animals like to live near people, too.

Come on a city safari. Find out if squirrels are living near you.

Why Do Squirrels Live in Towns and Cities?

Country squirrels live in woodlands with lots of big trees.

It can be hard for squirrels to find food in cold weather.

Towns and cities are warmer than the country. There are fewer **predators**.

Parks and backyards are full of treetop homes and tasty food.

What Makes Squirrels Good at Living in Towns and Cities?

Gray squirrels are not afraid to look for food near people.

If they **sense** danger, they climb to safety quickly.

Squirrels can climb very well.

Their curved claws grip things, and their tails help them steer as they jump from place to place.

Where Do Squirrels Rest and Sleep

Gray squirrels spend most of their time in trees.

They use leaves and twigs to build round nests called **dreys**.

They also build **dens** in warm places, such as hollow tree trunks and attics.

These high-up nests and dens are safe places to rest and sleep.

What Do Squirrels Eat?

Squirrels use their eyes and nose to find food on the ground.

Their sharp front teeth can crack open nuts, and nibble twigs and pinecones.

Squirrels also like fruit, seeds, buds, insects, bird eggs, and **fungi**.

They remember where to find tasty food, and visit these favorite places every day.

Why Do Squirrels Like Living Near People?

Backyards are full of snacks, such as bulbs, fish, fruit, and birdseed.

City squirrels often find more food than they can eat.

Squirrels dig small holes to bury extra nuts and seeds.

They sniff it out in winter, when there is less food around.

What Dangers Do Squirrels Face in Towns and Cities?

Gray squirrels can damage buildings with their strong teeth.

They can harm trees by tearing off the bark.

Many gray squirrels are trapped by people to stop them from doing damage.

In some places, people also hunt squirrels for food.

When Do Squirrels Have Babies?

Most squirrels **mate** twice a year, in May and December.

Look for males chasing females, making lots of noise!

The female lines a **drey** with soft things, such as moss, grass, paper, or **loft insulation**.

Three or four babies are born in the drey.

Why Is It Hard to Spot a Baby Squirrel?

The mother squirrel looks after her babies inside the **drey**.

After two months, the babies start to play outside, but they stay near the drey.

This makes it very hard to spot a baby squirrel.

After three months, the young squirrels leave and build dreys of their own.

Squirrel Spotter's Guide

Look back at the sights, sounds, and smells that tell you a squirrel might be nearby. Use these clues to go on your own city safari.

1 Look for squirrel footprints in mud or snow. Their front feet leave four claw marks, and their back feet leave five claw marks.

2 Try spotting a **drey** in winter, when trees have no leaves. The nests are the size of a football.

3 Squirrels are messy eaters. Look for nibbled shells or pinecones at the bottom of trees.

4 Squirrels make different noises. Listen for a clicking "kuk, kuk, kuk" alarm call, and the chattering sounds of males when it is time to **mate**.

Picture Glossary

den hidden home of a wild animal

drey squirrel's nest

fungi mushrooms and toadstools

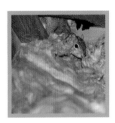

loft insulation material put into the loft of a house, to help keep the house warm

mate when a male and female animal get together to have babies

predator animal that hunts other animals for food

sense find out what is around through sight, hearing, smell, taste, and touch

...out More

Books

Owen, Ruth. *Squirrel Kits (Wild Baby Animals)*.
   New York: Bearport, 2011.

Zobel, Derek. *Squirrels (Backyard Wildlife)*.
   Minneapolis, Minn.: Bellwether Media, 2011.

Web sites

FactHound offers a safe, fun way to find Internet sites related to this book. All of the sites on FactHound have been researched by our staff.

Here's all you do:
Visit www.facthound.com
Type in this code: 9781432988098

Index

W9-DDL-984

TO THE RESCUE

adapted by Laura Driscoll
based on the original teleplay by Eric Weiner
illustrated by Dave Aikins

SCHOLASTIC INC.
New York Toronto London Auckland Sydney
Mexico City New Delhi Hong Kong Buenos Aires

One day Swiper the fox found a magic bottle. Inside the bottle was a dancing elf, who was determined to get out.

"Maybe I can trick this fox into freeing me!" the Elf said to himself. He knew that whoever opened the bottle would be magically pulled inside to take his place.

So the Elf begged Swiper to let him out. "I need lots of room to dance!" he said.

"Aw, poor guy," said Swiper. "He's stuck in there."

So Swiper opened the bottle. *Poof!* The Dancing Elf was free—but now Swiper was trapped inside!

Then the Elf went dancing off into the forest, leaving Swiper all alone.

"Oh Mannn!" moaned Swiper. "I need help. Maybe Dora and Boots can help me."

Swiper made his way to Dora and Boots and told them how the Dancing Elf had tricked him. "And now I'm stuck in here!" he cried.

"You poor fox," said Dora.
She started to open the bottle, but Swiper stopped her.
"If you open the bottle, *you'll* go in," he warned.
"Don't worry," Dora said. "We'll find a way to
get you out of this bottle. I promise."

Just then the bottle began to shake. It was dancing—and singing, too! The bottle told Dora, Boots, and Swiper that they would have to win one big wish.

"Where can we win one big wish?" asked Boots.

"If you make it to the Castle and win the King's dance contest, you'll win one big wish!" the bottle explained. "Then you could wish Swiper out of the bottle!"

Dora, Boots, and Swiper set off for the Castle right away. To get there, first they had to get through the Pyramid, which was guarded by the red Marching Ants. They wouldn't let Dora, Boots, and Swiper pass until they marched like Marching Ants.

 Will *you* help Dora, Boots, and Swiper march like Marching Ants? March, march, march!

The Ants were impressed—and they let Dora, Boots, and Swiper pass!

Farther along the path some Wiggling Spiders blocked their way. They wouldn't let Dora, Boots, and Swiper through until they wiggled like Wiggling Spiders . . .

 Wiggle your elbows! Wiggle your wrists! Dance like a Wiggling Spider!

. . . and the Spiders let them pass.

Finally Dora, Boots, and Swiper met up with some Sneaky Snakes. The Snakes wouldn't let them pass until they danced like snakes.

So Dora, Boots, and Swiper slithered and slid like the Sneaky Snakes . . .

 Put your hands over your head! Move them side to side! Slither like a Sneaky Snake!

and the Snakes let them pass. They made it through the Pyramid!

Next Dora, Boots, and Swiper made their way to the Ocean. There they met up with the Pirate Pig and his Pirate Piggies.

"We need to sail across the Ocean to win one big wish and free Swiper," Dora explained to them.

The Pirate Pig was happy to give them a ride across the Ocean on his pirate ship. But as they sailed, the waves got bigger and bigger. Suddenly a big wave washed Swiper and the magic bottle overboard! Before Dora could reach the bottle, a whale came up for air and—*gulp!*—he swallowed the magic bottle—Swiper and all!

Luckily, Backpack was carrying something that could make the whale sneeze: pepper!

"*Ah-choo!*" The whale sneezed a big sneeze. The bottle flew out of the whale's blowhole and back to safety on the pirate ship.

"That was fun!" Swiper said with a laugh. "I've never been sneezed by a whale before!"

As they sailed on, a Stormy Storm rolled in. The only way the Stormy Storm would let the ship pass was if everyone aboard did the Pirate Dance.

"That's our special dance!" said Pirate Pig. He and the Pirate Piggies started to dance, and Dora and Boots joined in . . .

Will *you* do the Pirate Dance? Rock your body from side to side! Swing your arms! Jump up and down! Clap your hands!

. . . and the Stormy Storm let them pass! They made it to the Castle just in time for the King's dance contest.

But the guard wouldn't let Dora and Boots into the Castle. "You have to wear fancy clothes!" he told them. "King's rules!"

Just then Benny floated by in his hot-air balloon with a bow tie for Boots and a fancy gown for Dora.

Dora and Boots were ready to dance! But the Dancing Elf was at the contest too. He wanted to win the one big wish for himself. And he *was* a good dancer!

King Juan el Bobo started the contest. "First you must do my favorite dance," he said. "The 'Ants in Your Pants' dance!"

Dora, Boots, and Swiper wiggled their hips like they had ants in their pants. So did the Dancing Elf.

Help Dora and Boots win the contest! Wiggle your hips like you have ants in your pants!

The King laughed. "Oh, that was very good," he told the dancers. But he wasn't ready to name a winner. He had another silly dance he wanted them to do. "To win one big wish," he said, "next you must dance like a fish!"

So everyone danced like a fish. They made fish faces. They flapped their arms like fish fins.

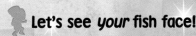 Let's see *your* fish face! Flap your arms like fish fins!

"*¡Excelente!*" said King Juan el Bobo. "You were all so good. I still can't pick a winner."

So the King gave the dancers the hardest challenge of all. "You must get my mommy to dance," he said. The King was sad that his mommy never danced.

"I'm just not good at it," said the King's mommy.

Dora had an idea. "We can do the 'Everyone Can Dance' dance," she said.

"Yeah," said Boots. "That dance gets *everyone* dancing!"

So Dora, Boots, and Swiper did the "Everyone Can Dance" dance!

Soon everyone was dancing—even the King's mommy!

Help get the King's mommy to dance! Do the "Everyone Can Dance" dance.
Put your hands on your hips! Shake your hips! Clap your hands! Jump up and down!

"You've done it!" said the King. "You got my mommy to dance! So I will give you one big wish! What do you wish for?"

Dora smiled. "I know what to wish for," she said. "I wish Swiper free!"

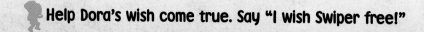 Help Dora's wish come true. Say "I wish Swiper free!"

Poof! In a swirl of sparkles Swiper was free!

The Dancing Elf was sorry that he tricked Swiper.

"I guess I have to go back into the bottle," he said sadly.

Dora asked the King if the Dancing Elf could stay out of the bottle. "He really loves to dance, and there's no room in there," she pointed out.

The King agreed—and declared that the Dancing Elf was to be free of the bottle forever! Everyone was thrilled. And do you know what they did to celebrate? They danced!